NATALIE'S RANCH HAND

SISTER BRIDES OF PEPPER GULCH

SUSANNAH CALLOWAY

Tica House
Publishing

Sweet Romance that Delights and Enchants!

PERSONAL WORD FROM THE AUTHOR

Dearest Readers,

Thank you so much for choosing one of my books. I am proud to be a part of the team of writers at Tica House Publishing who work joyfully to bring you stories of hope, faith, courage, and love. Your kind words and loving readership are deeply appreciated.

I would like to personally invite you to sign up for updates and to become part of our **Exclusive Reader Club**—it's completely Free to join! We'd love to welcome you!

Much love,

Susannah Calloway

VISIT HERE to Join our Reader's Club and to Receive Tica House Updates!

https://wesrom.subscribemenow.com/

CONTENTS

Personal Word From The Author   1

Chapter 1   4

Chapter 2   11

Chapter 3   21

Chapter 4   33

Chapter 5   43

Chapter 6   49

Chapter 7   60

Chapter 8   66

Chapter 9   75

Continue Reading…   81

Thanks For Reading!   84

More Mail Order Bride Romances for You!   85

About the Author   87

The roiling clouds heaved themselves across the skies, capping the plains of Pepper Gulch with an ever-changing mix of gray, white, and misty blue. There was a heat wave on the way, and the clouds weren't helping. Emory Spencer took a break from his work to stand up straight and give the skies a once-over; he dragged his forearm across his forehead, wiping away the sweat.

His boss, Ernest Flinn, looked over at him and grinned.

"Still getting adjusted to the weather here, after all this time?"

"I don't think that's it – it's been three years and besides, Colorado wasn't all that different from here in Utah."

"I guess anything different takes a little getting used to." Ernest was a kind-hearted man, and he didn't mind a bit that his foreman needed to take a minute to step into the shade. In fact, he put his own shovel down and accompanied him. "You wouldn't think it's only April, would you?"

Emory shook his head. "I remember growing up here, before Colorado – it never seemed like it got this hot this early. I reckon we're in for a bad summer."

"Especially with those clouds." Ernest nodded at the sky. "Tornados are rare around here, but when they do happen, they're not exactly a tempest in a teapot."

The skies did have a strangely eerie feel to them. Emory contemplated them for another moment and gave a little shiver.

"Twister came through in Colorado one year," he said. "Skies like this, that day, but we didn't know – we weren't expecting it. I remember Brigid was making supper, and I had stepped outside to fetch some water from the pump. I saw the twister form, away on the other side of the neighbor's barn." He shivered again. "Never seen anything like it. Never want to see anything like it again."

Ernest nodded, but seemed hesitant to speak. Emory realized that his boss was showing the care and sympathy that was habitual to him, stepping delicately around the mention of his wife, now gone these last three years…

He swallowed.

"Guess I don't mention Brigid much," he said.

"No, you don't."

Emory clenched his jaw a little.

"It's still difficult," he said. "But the more time that passes, the more I feel that I should speak about her. You know? As though avoiding her name is like pretending that she didn't exist. She and the baby, both."

"I know," said Ernest, quietly. Emory shot a glance over at him; the two were around the same age, had both grown up here in Pepper Gulch, and shared quiet, calm personalities. But the similarities did not end there. Ernest, too, had lost a wife, and had nearly lost his oldest daughter. The pain that Emory still felt, three years later, was undoubtedly still lodged in Ernest's heart.

But there was a difference between the two, Emory reckoned – Ernest had found love again. His wife Crystal was a delight, a sweet, caring woman, as perfectly suited to Ernest as anyone could imagine. The rancher's second marriage had brought joy to the tightly-knit community of Pepper Gulch – even if it had been a matter of writing for a Mail Order Bride.

Maybe that was what he himself ought to do, Emory thought ruefully. It wasn't as though he was likely to find anyone suited to him here in Pepper Gulch – or anyone that he was suited for, either, for that matter.

Then again, he didn't really mind being on his own. His life here on Flinn Ranch was quiet and calm – it fitted him perfectly. As foreman, he didn't have to sleep in the bunkhouse with the hands but had his own quarters in a neat little cottage behind the barn. The work was challenging but satisfying, and Crystal fed him supper at least twice a week. Besides that, in the last few years, he'd grown to have a close friendship with Ernest and his family – both those here and the relatives living about two hours away in South Meadows.

It was the happiest he'd been since Brigid had died, and he knew it.

Still, it was difficult to shake the feeling that there was something missing.

He pushed the thought out of his mind and returned to his work. Digging post holes for the new fence was going to take some time to finish off – he knew that his week was pretty much set. Here it was the middle of the week and bound to get hotter as the days went on. It wasn't an easy life, that was for sure – but the satisfaction of hard work well done, the time he spent with the Flinn family, it was all worth it.

The rest of the afternoon went by more swiftly than he could have imagined. By the time the sun drew close to the horizon, Emory felt the telltale twinges of his stomach. He was getting hungry – and suppertime was close. He and Ernest finished up the section of fencing they were working on and started the long walk back to the house. They could have been on horseback, but both men had agreed they enjoyed the leisurely walk in the early mornings, just as the sun was getting up. The long way back on foot at the end of the day was worth the joy of taking their time and moving through the refreshed, airy landscape of the morning.

As they approached the outbuildings, Ernest said, "Are you coming in for supper?"

"Well, I dunno. I sat down with you just two days ago – I hate to tarnish my welcome. Besides, Crystal and Daphne always have their hands full just keeping your little ones fed."

"Nonsense," said Ernest, waving a hand. "Crystal loves to have your company, and you know Ma doesn't mind a bit as long as you keep your elbows off the table. Besides, they made extra for tonight."

"Really? Why's that?"

"Mandy and all of them are on their way over. In fact," he said, squinting ahead of them in the direction of the ranch house, "it looks like they're arriving just about right now."

Emory followed his gaze. Sure enough, there was a wagon rolling up into the front yard, and it was recognizable as the one belonging to the York Ranch. No one else had a wagon that was painted bright red with blue trim– it was an eastern thing, Emory figured, and clear evidence of the influence Mandy and her sister-in-law Natalie had in the decisions of the everyday running of the ranch. Both the York siblings and the Chambers sisters had originally come from West Virginia, which seemed impossibly far away to Emory – he had never been any further east than Colorado. Now, Crystal Chambers was Crystal Flinn, and Mandy was Mandy York, and both young women were clearly as happy as could be in their new unions. It never failed to boggle Emory's mind, how folks could travel so far on a whim and a prayer, trusting that things would work out.

He supposed there was no real limit to how far you could go, with a need to believe and trust in God.

"Well, I dunno," he said again, feeling mixed emotions churn in his stomach. There was a strange, shy reluctance to insert himself into the family unit – and yet a strong yearning excitement, too. He loved to be surrounded by the Flinn-York family. As close as he was with Ernest and his own, he was equally drawn to the relatives that lived down in South Meadows. Perhaps even more so. Sweet Mandy, jovial Colin, energetic Anne, and Natalie…

As always, his brain seemed to stop in self-defense when he got to Natalie.

Colin York's sister was – well, she was something else. Of the three women from West Virginia, she had the strongest personality, had the most devoted drive to pursue her goals… and had the softest heart, he suspected. She had not shied away from him, though he was little more than a hired hand,

and she had given him the same respect that she gave everyone. She also gave him the what-for when he did something she considered foolish, but that, too, was the same what-for she gave everyone. Natalie did not do things by halves.

It was chiefly on her account, he knew, that he felt strangely shy about entering into the ranch house that evening.

Ernest clapped him on the back.

"If you dunno, I'll tell you," he said. "If you don't go and wash up this instant and present yourself for supper like usual, Crystal will tan your hide and use it for next season's rain boots. I don't reckon I can make it any plainer than that."

Emory laughed. "I reckon you're right, too. Okay, Ernest. I'll be over as soon as I'm presentable."

"If you're not, I'll send all three girls over to collect you, presentable or not."

His boss went on his way to the house, whistling a cheerful tune. Emory stood outside the entrance to his own living quarters, watching him go – and looking beyond him to see the figures emerge from the wagon, one by one. Tall Colin – slight Mandy – and the tall, forthright, willowy, graceful figure that belonged to Natalie York, with little Anne slung on her hip.

He bit his lip, watching from afar, then shook his head and went on into his cottage.

One of these days, he told himself, he'd have to get a handle on his confused feelings. Either they had to be done away with, or they had to be faced. One way or another, he had to move forward.

He wondered what lay ahead.

CHAPTER 2

Natalie York stepped down out of the wagon without the slightest bit of assistance, keeping her balance admirably despite the fact that Anne was hanging off her with both hands and trying desperately to get her mother's attention. Little Anne, as her uncle called her affectionately, wasn't quite so little anymore. As her child neared two years of age and became ever more demanding of her attention, Natalie could feel herself aging. She caught herself staring anxiously in the mirror each morning, certain that new lines and wrinkles were appearing overnight, carefully examining her thick blonde hair to see whether any silver strands were to be found among the gold…

It wasn't just the tiredness from helping to run the ranch and dealing with her adorable little energy-demander, of course. It was also the fact that her twenty-fifth birthday had just come and gone, and she was beginning to feel the weight of years pressing in on her.

Or perhaps it was the weight of Anne.

Now that they were safely on the ground, she put the squirming little girl down and watched her run toward the porch. Ernest's daughter Lina, ten years old and already a motherly young lady, bent down to take her into her arms, cooing eagerly at the little girl. The toddler and the older girl made nonsensical noises back and forth at each other as Lina carried her cousin into the house; Lina had long since recovered from the years she spent not speaking after the untimely death of her mother, who had been Ernest's first wife, but Lina still seemed to have a special affinity for creatures that didn't speak the language of the adults around her. If it wasn't baby talk with Anne, it was barks, growls, and whimpers with the ranch dogs, or a conversational whinny to any horse that happened by. It never failed to amuse Natalie, who considered herself to be quite normal but appreciated unique qualities in others.

Crystal, Lina's stepmother, watched the two run by with a fond smile, then turned that same affection on her sister and Natalie as they came up onto the porch. Colin waved at her and took the horse off to put him away in the stables. It was far later than the Yorks usually came for a visit – their ranch in South Meadows was two hours away, rendering most supper time visits difficult to carry out without traveling home late in the dark. But tonight was different; tonight, the whole family would stay over.

"I'm so glad you've made it," Crystal told them, pulling them one by one into a hug. "And what a treat to have you for the whole evening, and part of tomorrow besides. I've made up the bed in the spare room, and there's a cot for you and Anne in the kitchen, Natalie. Daphne was all set to give up her room…"

"Goodness, no." said Natalie. "I wouldn't hear of it. Poor Daphne needs her sleep."

Crystal scrutinized her for a moment.

"I would say that a young mother needs it, too," she said. "The good thing about the kitchen is its nice and warm all through the night and removed from the rest of us. I'm up with Simon all through the night, most of the time."

"Goodness, perhaps you and I ought to sleep in the kitchen, and we can let the men handle both Simon and Anne."

They chuckled, and Crystal pressed Natalie's shoulder in a sisterly way, leading them to the kitchen.

"I think I'd rather entrust Lina with Simon – Ernest is a devoted father, but he's a little too prone to falling asleep on the job. But Simon is six months old, now – I'm sure things will be getting easier from here on out."

Natalie had a great deal to say about that, but she decided, on reflection, that it was better to let her sister-in-law's younger sister hold onto hope.

They took seats around the kitchen table as Crystal went on fixing the last details of supper. Daphne, Ernest's mother, was already sitting in the kitchen in a rocking chair, holding little Simon. He was a good baby, Natalie thought, smoothing his fine, downy hair over his head. Quiet, calm, peaceful. Not a bit like Anne, as a matter of fact.

She had known when Anne was born that the little girl would be the adventure of a lifetime. She hadn't quite realized then just how much of an adventure it would be…

Pulling her thoughts away from that long-ago day, she refocused herself on the conversation that was being carried on in the kitchen.

"I'm glad that Colin felt comfortable enough with your new foreman to take a little holiday," Crystal was saying as she stirred something in a large pot on the stove. "After the disasters of the last two, I'm surprised at his confidence, I must say."

"Andrew has so far proven very trustworthy," said Mandy. "He's a little older than Oscar and Matthew were – a great deal more experienced, too. Besides, now that he's established, his wife will be coming out to stay with him, too, and we're going to hire her to help out around the house. It'll be better for all of us." She smiled a secretive little smile, one which Natalie didn't quite comprehend. For the last few weeks, it seemed that there was some unspoken secret in the York ranch house; but Natalie had put it down to Mandy and Colin being so newly wed, the sort of avid affection that belonged to hearts so clearly in tune. Now, in the light of the big kitchen at Flinn Ranch, she started to wonder whether there was something else to it.

She had just opened her mouth to ask a question when little Simon woke up and gave a cry. Daphne jiggled him on her shoulder for a moment, but with little effect; Crystal put her stirring spoon down and came to collect her son.

"Would you girls mind carrying things out to the table? I'll just give Simon his supper and then we'll be ready to eat."

Natalie and Mandy jumped eagerly into action. The supper that Crystal and Daphne had prepared together was wafting forth extremely appetizing smells; three of the household chickens had given their lives for the main course, and there were new potatoes, early greens from the garden, cooked apples, cornbread, wheat rolls, and gravy for any dish that seemed to need it. Led by the smell, no doubt, Lina found her way into the kitchen, Anne on her hip. Anne was already such a tall child and Lina was so small for her age, it was almost comical to watch them.

Natalie fought a chuckle as she lifted her daughter from the young girl.

"We've got to get this one a bib," she said. "I don't know if you've seen her eat lately, but she has no shame."

"She gets that from her uncle," said Colin, entering from the kitchen door and immediately taking the pan of cornbread away from his wife. "Don't go lifting anything too heavy, now."

"It's just cornbread," Mandy whispered to him, smiling.

"We take no risks in this family," he whispered back.

Natalie watched the whole exchange, feeling a strange excitement begin to bubble in her stomach. There was certainly a secret going on – and she had a feeling that it wouldn't be much longer before it was brought to light.

Before long, the supper was impressively spread out on the dining room table, and the family was gathering around it to eat. There was a lot of chatter going on – it had been over a month since the sisters had been together, and there was much news to be passed back and forth. Pepper Gulch and South Meadows were only some two hours away from each other, at opposite ends of the same county, but at times it seemed as though they might as well have been several states distant.

Pepper Gulch was the big town, though it was nothing compared to what they'd known back in West Virginia; South Meadows was so small that it did not yet have more than a tiny general store and a saloon. The general store was new, and Mandy and Natalie frequented it each week. For larger purchases, however, they still traveled the nineteen miles to Pepper Gulch's general store, which had a far larger selection as well as fabric goods.

Sometimes, when she felt stuck out in the middle of nowhere, Natalie resented how far away South Meadows was from her friends and civilization in general. Other times, when she remembered how lonely she had been even in the middle of a city in West Virginia, she was simply grateful for what she had.

Crystal returned, Simon in tow, and took her seat, completing the joint family unit. Ernest and Crystal, Daphne, Lina and Simon; Colin and Mandy, Natalie and Anne; no one was missing, and yet there was still one empty chair, situated just across the table from Natalie. Evidently, there was another guest, and Natalie had a suspicion of who it might be.

Her suspicion was confirmed when Crystal glanced out the window and said, with mock irritation, "Now, where is that man? You told him he was to come to supper, didn't you, Ernest?"

"I did," said Ernest easily. "I even warned him that you'd tan his hide if he didn't show. I can convey your threats just as well as you can, dear."

Colin started to laugh but tried to cut it off when Mandy shot him a look.

"There he is," said Lina quietly, pointing at the window.

A moment later, there was a hesitant knock on the door. Lina jumped from her seat and rushed to open it. She led the visitor down the hall and into the dining room, where he stood with his hands in his pockets for a moment, nodding and smiling a greeting to all.

"I thought we were going to have to take out after you, Emory," said Crystal. "Go on, take a seat." She smiled at him, despite her teasing, and the foreman responded in kind.

"Thank you for the invitation, Crystal," he said. "It's a pleasure to see all of you."

He sat down and his gaze swept across the table, one by one; when at last he came to Natalie, he allowed his gaze to linger. She smiled brightly at him and he smiled back.

"We're glad to see you too," she said.

His smile hitched even higher, and if she wasn't mistaken, he gave her a slight wink. Emory was a nice man, and she liked him. They hadn't spent much time together, but in the time they'd spent, she had come to consider him a friend. Besides, both her brother and Ernest had a genuine respect for him, and that was enough for her to trust him.

Trust wasn't easy after what had happened in her past – and she was relieved to find that she *could* trust again, though it cost her an effort.

"Well," said Colin, glancing at his wife, "I'm so pleased that we're all able to be here together. It seems as though it's been too long – and there's so much news to share."

Natalie sat up a little straighter, feeling as though the moment of truth were approaching. Was Colin about to confess what she suspected?

"For example," said Colin, clearing his throat, and giving his wife another secretive smile, "you'll all be pleased to know that we have a happy event in the offing…"

There were a few excited murmurs around the table. He waited just long enough for them to really get going before he said,

"Our prize pig will be having a litter any day now."

Ernest laughed outright, and Crystal reached over and pinched her brother-in-law.

"How dare you tease us like that."

Mandy was looking studiously at the tablecloth. She was, Natalie couldn't help but note, blushing as red as a beet.

"Of course, that's not the biggest news," Colin went on, rubbing his arm and grinning at Crystal. "Mandy and I are expecting our own little miracle – probably just one of them, though, not an entire litter."

His follow-up comment brought general laughter, but the laughter wasn't anywhere near as loud as the exclamations of delight and joy. Natalie felt her heart soar and then settle; just as she had suspected, her brother was going to have his own little one. He had always been so good with Anne; she knew that he would be an excellent father. And Mandy was the sweetest girl she'd ever known; she was bound to be a wonderful mother. Yes, their marriage, not quite a year old, was destined for happiness and blessings beyond measure.

That was what happened, she told herself, when someone who had been hurt learned to trust again. Colin, too, had been left in the dirt by someone he loved. His fiancée had gone off and married his best friend, years before. But he had learned to trust, and in trusting, he had learned to love.

It made her heart glow with warmth to see how things had turned out for her only sibling. She reached over to Colin and put a hand briefly on his, pressing warmly. Her older brother turned and gave her a genuine, overjoyed smile.

"Now I get to be an aunt," she said. "And you know what that means, don't you?"

"Oh, dear," said Colin.

She nodded. "That's right. I'm going to rile up your little one just before bedtime and let you bear the consequences. It's only fair after all the times with Anne."

He laughed, shaking his head, and she sat back in her chair, content to watch how happy her brother and his wife was. As she looked around the table, her eyes were drawn once more to Emory, sitting across from her. His mouth was stretched in a smile, to be sure – but there was something wrong. The smile had not reached his eyes, and there was a sadness in them that hurt her heart to see. He was glad on behalf of the others – but he was sad on his own behalf.

What could have triggered such an expression at a time like this?

Mystified, she found that she was watching him closely, more closely than she had ever looked at her friend before. Though his eyes were sad, there was still a lively warmth in them; he was hatless, and his dark hair fell sharply across his forehead, his face already tanned from the sun. She realized suddenly that she had rarely seen a more handsome man than Emory Spencer.

Suddenly, feeling the weight of her gaze, his eyes flickered over to meet hers. The connection felt like a jolt to her stomach; it was only by the force of her will that she kept herself from looking away immediately. Their eyes stayed fixed on each other for the space of a few breaths, and when finally, she dragged her gaze away, she found that her heart was pounding.

It was unexpected – and one of the more exciting things that had happened to her since she came to Utah.

She wondered what it meant – and had a sinking feeling she already knew.

CHAPTER 3

The next few days after the visit to Flinn Ranch and the exciting announcement passed in a flurry of activity. According to the new foreman of York Ranch, spring was always a busy time on a cattle ranch.

"In fact," Andrew said, pushing his hat back on his head, "I don't reckon that there's any time on a cattle ranch that isn't busy – leastways, not if you're doing it right."

Natalie was grateful for Andrew's presence. Their first foreman, Oscar Bowden, had been a disgrace and had actively acted against the interests of the York siblings when they came to take over their grandfather's ranch. The one that came after him, Matthew Allen, was scarcely any better. Now, she was glad to find that the third time was indeed the charm; Andrew was in his forties, solid, steady, and loyal. He had been at York Ranch for a month, and everything was already running like clockwork.

His wife Melissa arrived the day after the family returned from Flinn Ranch. Now that Natalie knew the truth about

Colin and Mandy expecting, it made even more sense that they would bring an extra pair of hands into the house. And Melissa had proved to be just as useful as her husband; within a short time, Natalie found that she had plenty of time to look after Anne, and after her sister-in-law as well, as Mandy began to feel the ill effects of pregnancy.

On the first morning that she took sick, Natalie sat by her bed and held her hand. Colin was already out in the fields with Andrew, and Anne was being uncharacteristically quiet and good, obviously worried about her auntie.

"I hope you make it through this ordeal more easily than Crystal did," Natalie observed, patting Mandy's hand. "She had a hard time of it all the way through, if I recall correctly."

Mandy chuckled weakly. "Poor Crystal – well, she was younger than I am, and smaller. I reckon things'll run a little more smoothly for me."

"I hope so." Natalie squeezed her hand comfortingly. "Even if we bring Amy in to help out a few times a week again, I don't know that I'll be able to keep everyone fed and happy without you. So you just concentrate on feeling the best that you can, as quick as you can."

"I will," said Mandy softly. Her eyes were fluttering closed, and it was obvious that she needed to rest.

Natalie patted her once more, then took Anne by the hand and led the toddler out of the door, closing it softly behind her.

"Is Auntie sick?" whispered Anne loudly.

"She just needs to sleep, dear."

"Where's Lina?"

"At her own house, of course, silly goose."

"Can we go see her?"

"Not today. Soon, perhaps."

"Can we go see her tomorrow?"

Natalie sighed. Once Anne got on this line of questioning, there was no stopping her – unless she acted quickly to distract her.

"How would you like to go outside and pick wildflowers in the yard?" she suggested. "We can take some bread and feed the ducks and chickens, too."

"I want to feed bread to the f'owers," said Anne, folding her chubby little arms with determination. Natalie looked down at her daughter and laughed, shaking her head.

"If your uncle could see you right now, he'd say, *She gets that from me*," she told her. "But he'd be wrong – you are one hundred percent Little Natalie." She swooped the girl up, though it strained her back, and jogged her through the house and out the front door. The only way to make sure that Anne followed through on what she was told was to put her right smack dab in the middle of it, and so she plopped the little girl down in the yard, square on her bottom, plucked a daisy and hastily thrust it into her little fist.

"Like this, Annie – see how pretty?"

Anne did indeed see how pretty, and she was distracted immediately, as her mother had hoped. Natalie sat down cross-legged next to her daughter, not caring in the least how unladylike she must look; it wasn't as though there was anyone around to see, after all.

She watched her daughter as the little girl enthusiastically began picking everything she could reach, whether flowers or simple blades of grass. The serious contemplation on her face was also a very York trait – but with each day that passed, as Anne got older, Natalie could see a little more of the child's father in her. Oh, it wasn't easily seen by anyone who hadn't known Timothy Clark, but to Natalie, it was painfully obvious. The color of Anne's clear amber eyes, the firm set of her chin, even the wideness of her shoulders all spoke of the influence of Timothy Clark on her heritage.

And it made Natalie feel as though heartbreak was moving closer with every day.

Would she ever look at Anne and not think of how Timothy had behaved? How he had convinced her – seduced her – and fled as soon as his responsibilities had caught up with him?

She shook her head, watching Anne put together a haphazard bouquet.

Natalie should think of the good things, she knew. There had been pleasant times with Timothy Clark – she had fallen in love with him, after all. They had worked at the same factory; he was a foreman, and she was a humble laborer, doing her best to help her older brother keep their family afloat. That was before their mother had died, of course; once Christine York had passed away from her long illness, the debts she'd left on her children had to be quickly dissolved. But Natalie continued to work; she liked to work. She liked to feel useful, appreciated.

Timothy had made her feel both of those things – at first.

They were engaged when Natalie had finally given in to him; at least, he had told her they were engaged. But he didn't want her to announce it to anyone else. Looking back on it from three years later, Natalie felt sorry for that innocent girl who had believed everything she had been told.

It wasn't until long after Timothy left and fled West Virginia that she found out he'd been officially engaged for years to a girl from his hometown, an old family friend. His life had been planned out for him from the time he was fifteen.

Now, looking back on his actions as well, she could muster up a little pity for him. Yes, he had acted selfishly; and yes, he had behaved like a cad and a coward. But he must have been frightened, too, just like she had been when she realized she had been deserted. He was the same age as she was. He had little experience in the ways of the world.

The only thing he had that she didn't was a gift for sweet-talking others into doing what he wanted them to do.

She wondered idly what had ever happened to him…and surprised herself by finding that she wished him no ill will. No, the years since he left her had not been easy. Anne was not easy. Raising a child as an unwed mother certainly was the most painful and difficult thing she had ever done. But Natalie had her brother, and she had Anne.

As awful as things had been, she couldn't help but feel that she had gotten the better end of the deal. Here she was, hundreds and hundreds of miles away from the place of her birth, helping to run a ranch. She had a family, and friends, and her whole life ahead of her – even though some days she felt as though the better part of it was left behind.

She spotted the figure of her brother, approaching from the far fields. He walked with his hands in his pockets and his head up, whistling a tune.

Natalie waved at him, and he waved back, making his way over to join her. He plopped himself down in the grass next to her and gave her a grin.

"Making flower crowns today?"

"Trying to keep Anne away from your poor wife. She's sleeping."

Colin's eyebrows drew together immediately in concern. "She's ill?"

"Don't look so worried." Natalie shoved at his shoulder playfully. "It's to be expected in her condition. You remember how I was for the first few months."

He nodded uncertainly. "I was worried to death – and somehow it doesn't seem like it'll be any easier with my wife than it was with my sister."

"Mandy is strong. She'll be fine. By the time you have your little one in your arms, it'll all be forgotten."

This wasn't entirely true, she thought ruefully; she could remember her own sickness quite vividly. But it needed to be said, if only to help her brother to relax.

And relax a little he did, doubling his knees up and looping his arms around them. He squinted into the distance.

"Someone's turning onto our lane."

"How can you see that far away?"

"Maybe you need spectacles, Natalie."

"Don't be ridiculous," said Natalie, shoving at him again and trying to see what he was seeing. It was true, her eyesight was a bit dimmer than his – but she wasn't about to get spectacles. She was worried enough about looking older than her age as it was.

Colin, with the acuteness of all older brothers, said, "Squinting will give you wrinkles, you know."

"Oh, psshh."

This earned him another shove, which he bore with brotherly amusement, grinning at her.

The faraway figure had come close enough for her to see clearly, and even to recognize.

"Why, surely that's Emory Spencer. What's he doing all the way out here?"

"And on a horse, too, not in the cart – he's alone."

"Oh, I do hope nothing has happened to Lina or Simon." Natalie twisted her hands together. Colin patted them comfortingly.

"He's not riding fast. I don't imagine he's got any pressing news – just looks like a neighborly visit, from what I can tell."

"From two hours away?"

"You're right, that seems a little far…" Colin shot her a swift, teasing glance. "Maybe it's a little more than neighborly. Maybe it's the prelude to a courtship."

"Oh, Colin, control yourself, please."

"I mean it. It's obvious that he's taken a shine to you. Why, when we were over there for supper, he could hardly keep his eyes from you."

His teasing was irritating – and embarrassing, too, somehow. She couldn't help but blush; and because he was her brother, he couldn't help but comment on it.

"What's this? Maidenly blushing? Is there something I should know, Nat?"

"Don't be ridiculous. Emory and I are just friends, and that's all."

"If you say so, Natalie. But just you remember it – Emory's my friend, too. He's a good man, and I like him."

Irked, she stared hard at him. "And?" she said.

"And," said Colin, grinning, "be nice to him."

She hadn't time to say anything else before Emory was within earshot, so she lapsed into fuming about her brother's comments. She knew that he had only said them to get under her skin, and by golly, he had succeeded. The result was that, as Emory rode up, she knew that both her greeting and her expression lacked warmth.

By the shy, uncertain way he responded, she knew he had noticed.

Ignoring the hand that Colin held out to assist her to her feet, she pushed herself up to a stand, and forced herself not to fold her arms defensively.

"What brings you all the way out here to South Meadows, Emory?" she said. "I trust that nothing is wrong at Flinn Ranch."

"No, no, everything's fine. Matter of fact, I'm here to deliver a little care package from Miss Crystal, for Miss Mandy." He fumbled in the saddle bag and handed over a paper-wrapped packet. "Not sure what all she sent, but she said something about a ginger tea that helped her feel better when she was expecting."

Colin reached out to accept the packet.

"Many thanks, Emory – but Crystal really sent you all this way just to bring us some ginger tea? Her care as a sister is exemplary, but her reasonableness as an employer could use a little fine tuning."

"Well, she didn't need to send me, exactly," said Emory. "I sort of volunteered."

He was clearly trying to keep his gaze on Colin, but it kept getting away from him and slipping over to Natalie instead. She blushed deeply, to her chagrin, surely turning so scarlet that she could practically feel the vitality of the color.

"It's been a long time since I've come out this way, anyhow," he said. "I don't want to lose my feel for the county."

"Goodness knows," said Colin, with a veneer of politeness that hid his teasing tone only thinly. "It would be terrible to lose your feel...for the county."

Natalie elbowed him sharply, and he grinned at both of them.

"I'll take this on in to Mandy and fix her up a cup. Will you stay for dinner, Emory?"

"Thanks, Colin, but I've got to head back. I appreciate the invitation."

"We'll see you around, then."

"Sure will. Thanks."

Emory made no move to leave; Colin left immediately. Anne, who had been watching everything with the avid, eager eyes of a youngster who has no understanding of anything she's hearing but has drawn her own conclusions, scrambled up from her place in the dirt and ran to Emory's horse.

"Anne."

"Don't worry, Miss Natalie," said Emory, swinging down from his horse and picking the little girl up right away. "I've got her."

"Up," said Anne, pointing regally to the horse. Holding her in one arm, Emory obliged, putting himself back in the saddle and setting her in front of him. He held on to Anne with both hands; Natalie was still inclined to be leery of horses, and especially when it came to their interactions with her little daughter. But as she watched Emory hold Anne to the little girl's heart's content, she realized that she had never felt so trusting of another human being and their ability to care for her daughter.

She swallowed hard, stepping forward.

"I suppose all of Pepper Gulch is preparing for the spring dance," she said. Why in the world had she brought that up? Goodness, but he would think her forward.

Emory's eyes fixed on hers, that same firm, meaningful gaze that she remembered from the other night at supper; the weight behind it made her heart beat faster still.

"Sure is," he said. "I hope you and yours are planning to attend again this year."

"Wouldn't dream of missing it," she said. "I love to dance."

"Yeah – I remember that." He nodded, giving her a smile full of meaning. She wondered if he remembered last year's dance for the same reasons she remembered it so clearly.

"I expect you've got your dance card full already," she said, surprised at the words as they emerged from her mouth.

"Me? No, ma'am. I don't intend to dance at all."

"That's what you said last year, and yet you danced with me more than once."

"That's different," said Emory quietly.

"Is it? Now that everyone knows you're such a good dancer, you'll be fending the girls off with a stick."

He chuckled.

"I don't reckon that's even a little bit true, any of what you just said," he told her. "But I'd be happy to dance with you, Natalie, if that's what you're aiming for." His words took her breath away, and their eyes met once more. Emory visibly fumbled for something to dilute the tension between them and found it in Anne. "And of course, Annie here, if she's old enough to attend this year."

"She would love it," said Natalie wistfully, looking at her little girl. "She dances all day long. I can't imagine what she'll think of hearing music along with it."

"I reckon attending her first dance will be a memory she'll treasure," said Emory.

Natalie steeled herself to meet his gaze.

"I reckon so, too," she said.

He lifted Anne from off the saddle and handed her down to Natalie.

"Guess I'd better get on back home. A few weeks yet until the dance, Natalie – I'll see you there."

"I look forward to it," she blurted out, before she knew quite what she was going to say. He was in the middle of turning his horse around, and facing away from her, but she caught a flare of color on his sun-tanned cheeks. She had made him blush the way he made her blush.

Why did that feel like such a triumph?

Whatever the reason, she thought, three weeks suddenly seemed like a very long time.

CHAPTER 4

"Emory."

Emory was startled out of his reverie by someone calling his name. Realizing he had been staring into the distance for the last several minutes – rather than finishing combing out the horse's mane, as he was meant to be doing – he stepped back from his work, feeling rather guilty. But it was Daphne who stood in the door of the barn, and she didn't seem to realize that anything had been amiss.

Ernest Flinn's mother was a spunky older lady, with just as much pep and vigor as her daughter in law, and somehow even more than her sweet, quiet granddaughter Lina.

"I hate to ask this of you," Daphne said, coming toward him, hands clasped in front of her. "I know you just got back from your ride to South Meadows – but Crystal and I are putting supper together for tonight, and she realized that we're almost out of flour. I came up with a few other things that we could use, too. Would you mind riding Racer back into Pepper Gulch and going to the general store? Of course, we'll make it worth your while," she added. "You're invited to supper, naturally."

Emory smiled at her. It was mid-afternoon, and the ride to and from South Meadows had been a swift one. He was a little tired out from the jaunt – but the journey itself had felt more than worth it, just to see the smile and the faint blush on the face of Natalie York when he had arrived. He wasn't sure just why that felt like such an accomplishment, but it certainly put him in a good mood.

"I don't mind at all," he said. "It won't take more than fifteen minutes to ride into Pepper Gulch. I'll swing by the post office while I'm there. I've been meaning to do that this week anyhow."

"Oh?" Daphne's eyebrows arched, and she looked at him keenly. "Expecting something good?"

"Expecting a wedding invitation, actually. My little sister Almira's been seeing her fellow for a few months now, so I've been anticipating hearing wedding bells for a while."

"Almira – yes, I remember her. She was so young when your folks moved away. Hard to believe that she's old enough to get married now."

"Eighteen last December," said Emory proudly. "Though I don't guess she'd like to hear me say it – women don't like other people to know their ages, do they, Miss Daphne?"

Daphne laughed.

"Some of them are more sensitive than others, I guess," she said. "Myself, I was sixty-three in November, and I'm grateful for every day that I've got."

"That's how I feel," said Emory, glad to have an understanding ear. "Life isn't easy, and not everyone has the privilege of growing old. We should celebrate every day we're given."

Daphne put a hand on his shoulder.

"Emory Spencer, you're a deep and poetic soul underneath it all, aren't you? No wonder you spend so much time alone – you're the type to contemplate life, to think about things, not just roll over them and move on." She gave him a motherly smile. "I reckon that's why you and my son get along so well. You're alike as two peas in a pod. I'm sure I don't need to tell you how happy Ernest and Crystal were to hear that you moved back to Pepper Gulch and were willing to come and work on the ranch. You're the kind of help we all need, steady and peaceful. And a good friend, besides."

Emory chuckled.

"You don't need to keep flattering me, Miss Daphne – I already said I'd ride in for your supplies. In fact, I'd better head out now if you want them back in time to fix supper." He reached for the saddle and tack again.

Daphne chuckled a little herself.

"Right you are. Here's our list – we'll get ready what we can and fix the rest when you get back. Be careful, son."

Her casual familiarity and affection with him made his heart glow a little. He missed his family, he realized – his parents, far away in Colorado, and his sister. He'd followed them out there years ago, after holding down his first adult jobs here in Pepper Gulch, making deliveries all over the county. And that was where he had met Brigid…

He could remember it as clearly as though it were yesterday. Setting foot in the church that first Sunday morning after arriving in Colorado, a little later than he should have been but scrubbed clean and dressed in his Sunday best. The congregation was too well-trained to turn and look at him as he had made his way toward the pew where his parents and younger sister stood, singing the hymns. It was only when he had taken his place at the end of the row that the young woman in the row just in front of him had turned, revealing a pretty face and the widest blue eyes he'd ever seen. She had looked him up and down, held a finger to her lips to shush him, and then given him a wink. That wink had sealed his fate; Emory had been even more shy and awkward then than he was now, all these years later. To be winked at by a pretty girl was enough to make him practically fall into his seat when the singing was over and it was time to sit down; he'd never felt so weak in the knees, so dizzy. He entertained the momentary thought that he might actually be ill.

Everything that had happened since then – the shy and fumbling courtship, the joyful day of the wedding, a few years of utter bliss, the news that they were expecting a baby...

And then the horrible day that things had gone so terribly, and no one had been able to stop it or prevent it or fix it...

In the space of twelve hours, he had gone from a happy, hopeful family man to losing his wife and unborn child to a sickness that no one had been able to explain, not even the doctors. There was some weakness in Brigid, somehow; the thought had been impossible to Emory. Brigid had been the strongest woman he'd ever known.

The memories washed over him like a tide and left him reeling. As he came back to himself, he realized he was on the horse and halfway to Pepper Gulch. The sun was sinking low, approaching the horizon. He'd have to hurry if he wanted to get back before it was pitch black outside.

He put his heels to the mare, desperate to outrun the sun and his own dark thoughts.

What he needed was a distraction, he told himself – and so, while Mr. Parmeter at the general store wrapped up the items on Daphne's neatly written list, Emory checked in at the post office to see whether he had any mail waiting for him. He did, indeed, an envelope marked with the clear, decisive hand that he recognized as belonging to Almira. His joy at receiving communication from his family and his anticipation of what the letter might hold faded quickly once he opened it.

He read it through once and then again, growing in disbelief – and in sadness and anger.

Dear Emory –

Well, I suppose you're expecting to hear from me that our engagement is official. And I wish I could tell you that it is so. Up until yesterday, I could have. But today, everything changed...

Impossible as it seemed, his little sister's husband-to-be had been unfaithful to her. Emory's outrage and anger only grew as he read Almira's words of regret and sadness. She was such a tough little thing; it was evident that she was trying to hide the depth of her feelings from her big brother. But he could see through it, and his protectiveness of her only grew. John Elwood had promised himself to Almira Spencer – and had gone back on his promise. Almira was left heartbroken and alone, and her destroyed love bled through every word of her letter.

Fuming and unsure of what to do with this sudden burden of anger – he was not a man who was easy to anger, usually, but doing this to his only sister was certainly a prime way to go about it – he collected the packages from the general store, stowed them in the saddlebags, and started along the ride home. As his mind reeled, going over and over the letter she had sent, the trip went by swiftly, and before he knew it, he was thundering into the yard at Flinn Ranch.

He put the mare away and stalked toward the ranch house, still trying to grasp what he had been told. His upset was apparently obvious; he had hardly set foot in the kitchen before Crystal gave a little cry.

"Goodness, Emory. What's wrong?"

He glanced up at her, setting the packages down on the table. Immediately, he felt a bit ashamed of himself; if his anger was that obvious, it probably meant that he had been less than polite to Mr. Parmeter and George at the post office, too.

"I got a letter from my sister Almira."

"Oh, dear – is everything alright?"

"Not exactly, no." He hesitated. "I don't rightly know that I should talk about it much. I might end up swearing."

Crystal half-chuckled and pulled a chair out at the kitchen table for him. "Come on, Emory. We're all friends here. You're upset – tell us what's going on, and I'll make you some tea."

She put the kettle on and began to unpack the supplies he had brought; Daphne brought Simon over, deposited him in Emory's arms, and then took the flour he'd brought back and began to make pie crust with Lina's help. Ernest, too, appeared from nowhere; with his usual tact, he seemed to understand that something was afoot, and simply sat down at the table next to Emory, giving him an encouraging smile.

Sitting there in the cozy kitchen, holding the sleeping baby and watching the Flinn women bustle around him busily, Emory's shoulders began to relax as the anger drained away.

"Well, here are the facts of it," he said. "My poor little sister, just eighteen years old, has been courted by a ranch hand in Tin City, Colorado. She's never been courted before, and she fell head over heels for this fellow, as far as I can tell – which is ironic, because he turned out to be quite a heel himself." He shook his head. "Up and ran off with some other girl, not two weeks after he asked her to marry him."

"That's terrible." cried Crystal. "The poor girl – why, she's only a year younger than me. Can you imagine?" she appealed to her husband. "The poor thing."

"A sad story," said Ernest, shaking his head. "I wish it were the only one I'd ever heard like that, but the fact is that there are more dishonorable men than I like to think of in this country."

Daphne shook her head and clucked disapprovingly.

"Poor girl," murmured Lina, caught up more in her stepmother's reaction than her own understanding of what had occurred. Despite himself, Emory couldn't help but smile at the young girl's display of empathy for something for which she had no clear comprehension. Empathy wasn't about understanding, he thought; it was about compassion even without understanding.

It was a shame that Almira wasn't here, surrounded by good folks like these...

The thought triggered something in him, and he pulled the letter out of his pocket and opened it again, quickly scanning through. He'd missed it on his first two times of reading it, as he had been so upset by the contents. But now it was finally sinking in.

He looked up slowly at Ernest.

"How, uh – how would you feel about having a guest on the ranch?"

"Does she want to come here?" Ernest asked, picking up on his meaning right away.

"Well, as a matter of fact, I reckon she's already on her way. This letter is dated last week – I haven't been to the post office for a while. She said she was going to come for a visit, and that she'd get a room in a boarding house."

"Nonsense," said Crystal immediately. "Why should she stay in a boarding house when she's got family here?"

"I had a feeling you'd feel that way," said Emory gratefully. "If she stays in the boarding house, she won't be able to stay for more than a few days. But I can put her up in my bed and sleep in my kitchen…"

"That little cottage isn't near big enough for you and your sister," said Daphne practically. "We've got a spare room here – why doesn't she just stay with us? You'll never be far away, and you can take all your meals with us while she's here."

Emory glanced over at Ernest, who nodded.

"Are you sure? That's a lot to ask."

"Nonsense," said Crystal, even more stoutly this time. "We'll look forward to the company, won't we, Daphne?"

"Of course, we will."

Emory relaxed into a smile,

"Well, thank you all. That's a relief to me – I know she'll be happier here than she would be in the boarding house. I don't know how long she'll want to stay…"

"As long as she likes," said Ernest. "I reckon she just needs some time away from home, and to see her big brother, too. She and Lina will get along, too, won't you, Lina?" His daughter nodded emphatically.

"And she'll be here for the party," put in Crystal. "The spring dance. If that doesn't put some color back into her world, I don't know what would."

Emory nodded.

"She does love to dance," he said. "Almost as much as…as Miss Natalie, I reckon."

"Then that's settled," said Crystal, dusting her hands off as though she had accomplished a particularly difficult task. "Come on, Lina, let's set the table. Supper in five minutes. Pie will be done shortly after we eat. Ernest and Emory – consider yourself notified."

Emory looked at his employer, who gave him a kindly smile and clapped him on the shoulder.

"We're sorry for your sister," he said. "I reckon most people know what it feels like to lose someone that you love, whether from betrayal or to the cruelties of time and illness. But we'll do our best to put a smile on her face again while she's here. Nobody that young should have to deal with a hurt like that."

Emory nodded. "Thanks, Ernest," he said. "It means a lot to me."

Ernest squeezed his shoulder and stood up.

"What are friends for? Come on, you." He took his little son from Emory's arms. "I'm starving."

CHAPTER 5

Reckoning by the date on his little sister's letter and the date that she suggested she would be catching a train to head toward Pepper Gulch, it was only a few days later that Emory hitched the horse to the wagon and headed into town to meet Almira. He was fairly sure he was guessing the right arrival date. Traveling to Pepper Gulch from her area of Colorado wasn't simple; it required some time on a train, and then a switch to a stagecoach. By the time she arrived, he suspected, she would be exhausted.

But as upset as she had been, he also suspected, even the exhaustion would be a welcome distraction.

A coach arrived twice a day, once around noon and then later in the evening. He timed it to arrive in town in time for the noon coach, hoping that she would be early. To his delight, he arrived outside the stage stop just as the coach itself was pulling up. Not many people disembarked at Pepper Gulch to stay, but there were a handful of them who took advantage of the opportunity to get out and stretch their legs, catch a bite to eat at the inn, or do a little sight-seeing. Among the travelers was a young woman who did not even quite look her eighteen years; she had thick dark hair, much like Emory's, and wide dark eyes. She was plainly, even conservatively dressed by Pepper Gulch standards; even in the warmth of the spring day, she had a shawl wrapped around her shoulders. She gripped a small valise in one hand and watched anxiously for some sign of a familiar face.

It touched his heart to see the smile that broke over her face like the dawn when she finally spotted him, coming forward out of the crowd.

"Emory."

"Almi," he said, reaching out to pull her into his arms. He held her tightly, surprised at the strength of the emotion he felt. He hadn't seen her in three years, after all – not since the funeral for his wife. He had left Colorado right after the last shovelful of dirt was put in place, unable to face the depth of his sadness and desperate to run from his emotions.

He reckoned that his sister felt very similarly.

He put her at arm's length and looked her up and down.

"Well, look at you. When I saw you last, you were still a kid. What happened?"

"Life," she said, laughing and shaking her head.

"If you look this different, I can't imagine what I must look like to you – an old man, I guess."

"Nonsense." She tucked her arm through his as they began to walk away from the stagecoach. "You look exactly the same – other than your hair's a little longer. Don't you have a barber in this town?"

"Yeah, sure, but I never go to him."

She laughed again and elbowed him in the side in a very little-sister manner.

"Pepper Gulch. It's been so long since I was here, I wonder if I'll remember any of it."

"I dunno, you weren't much more than five or six when you and Ma and Pa took off for Colorado."

"I know, I know. I cried all the way, do you know that? I couldn't believe that we had left you behind."

"Well, I was working, had a place of my own. I was practically a grown man."

"You were younger then than I am now."

"Ahh, see, just goes to show the difference between you and me, doesn't it?"

She smiled up at him happily. "I can't believe that it's been so long…"

"I know."

"So much has happened, Emory…so much has gone…has gone wrong…" Suddenly her smiles turned to tears, and her emotions broke through to show on her face. Her grip on his arm tightened. "I don't know how to even talk about it. I don't know how to explain…"

"That's all right," he said gently. He stopped and turned her to face him, taking hold of her shoulders. Looking down at her face, he was overwhelmed with love and reflected pain; he pulled her toward him and kissed her forehead. "It's a difficult thing to lose someone you love," he told her. "No matter how it happens."

"I know...I know you went through it with Brigid." She hiccupped and wiped at her eyes with her sleeve, looking even younger than she usually did. "And I know what happened with me and – and John..." She could scarcely even pronounce his name. "I know it doesn't even begin to compare..."

He shook his head, reaching down to take her hands in his.

"Don't compare," he said. "Never compare. Every pain you go through is unique and your own, and no less important than anyone else's. No more so than your happiness is more or less important than anyone else's. I'm so sorry for what he's done to you, Almi – but believe me when I tell you that it will get better. Time will heal the wounds. You may never lose the scars, but you'll be stronger for them." He waited patiently until she got ahold of herself, stopped sobbing, and looked up at him.

"Is that how you feel?" she said. "Stronger for the scars? Better with time?"

He nodded. "Yes," he said, and as he said it, he knew suddenly that it was true. Three years had

gone by since he had lost Brigid and the baby, and it wasn't as though he never thought of them – he thought of them every day. But the pain had faded, just as scars fade. He carried their memory close to his heart, but they were no longer in front of him constantly, obscuring his vision. He was starting to see his future, now.

She was still sniffling, but he could tell that she was ready to focus on something else other than her own unhappiness.

He gave her an encouraging smile.

"The good news is," he said, "I don't have to take you to the boarding house and leave you there to get along by yourself. Ernest and Crystal Flinn have invited you to come and stay with all of us on the ranch."

"Oh, Emory, really?"

He nodded. "They're good people – you'll like them. And they have a little boy, just six months old, just about old enough to play with. Lina's a sweetheart, too, you'll love her. And Daphne is a mother to all of us. You won't be neglected."

"As long as you'll be there, too."

"I'll be right next door."

He tucked her arm back through his, took a firm grip on her valise, and walked her toward the inn.

"But before we head back to the ranch, I suggest that we go and have something to eat. The Pepper Gulch Inn is famous for its hush puppies."

"That sounds like exactly what I need…and…Emory…thank you for letting me come here to stay with you. I simply needed to get away for a while."

"I thought you might," he said, nodding. "Besides, 'letting you' might be stretching it a little…after all, you more or less invited yourself."

"Emory!"

"Wasn't as though I could say no, now, was it?"

He was teasing her, and she knew it. He reckoned she missed it; there was something about being teased by a sibling that was almost comforting.

She laughed and tugged on his arm.

"I guess that's so," she said. "Not that you would have said no, in any case. Come on, Emory – I'm starving, and I'm desperate for some tea."

"Right you are, Almi."

He led her into the inn, feeling strangely comforted by how easy it was to comfort his sister. Maybe he was a better big brother than he'd ever given himself credit for.

Or maybe it was just more proof of the fact that what people in pain really needed was a listening ear.

CHAPTER 6

"Only a week until the spring dance," wailed Mandy, holding up her favorite dress. "How on earth am I going to go if I can't fit into any of my clothes?"

It was a fact that Mandy Chambers York had grown quite a bit recently, especially around the midsection. Natalie didn't recall growing quite so quickly when she herself had been pregnant; but then, she was taller and slimmer than Mandy, and perhaps she hadn't really been paying attention to that aspect of her pregnancy, anyhow. She'd had other things to occupy her mind…

Pushing the bad memories away, she took the dress from Mandy and scrutinized it, eyeing the difference in circumference between the garment and Mandy's burgeoning belly.

"Do you think we can alter it?" Mandy asked her.

Natalie shook her head.

"Even if I did today, by the time Saturday rolls around it probably wouldn't fit any more. I can't take enough out to ensure that it'll be wearable for more than a few days at the rate you're going."

"Oh, dear," said Mandy, wringing her hands. "I should have thought of this earlier."

"You're not to blame – it isn't as though you've ever been pregnant before, after all. I should have thought to warn you, but you're growing so fast… whoever is in there is going to be a strong, vibrant child, that's for certain." She bent slightly to call to the infant within. "If you could just slow things down a little…"

"Oh, Natalie," said Mandy, putting her hands over her belly protectively and chuckling. "You know I'm not really complaining. Everything about having a child is wonderful, but…"

"Nonsense," said Natalie briskly. "Not everything about having a child is wonderful. Plenty about it is painful, uncomfortable, or downright embarrassing." She gave her sister-in-law a sweet smile. "It's just that once you have the baby in your arms, you forget all about that. Now, what can be done about this particular problem?"

"Do you suppose I could borrow a dress from someone… Amy, perhaps?"

"No, you really need clothing that will last for the next several months, not just temporary hand-me-downs. Besides, Amy's taller than you." Natalie tapped her finger to her lips. "There's nothing for it, I'm afraid. We'll have to drive to Pepper Gulch and see what the general store has in the way of ready-made clothing."

"Do you think they'll have something that will work?"

"If it doesn't fit right, we can alter it. But we're going to have to start with something much larger than what you usually wear, if you want it to last."

Mandy chewed on her lower lip for a moment thoughtfully. "You're right," she said. "Pepper Gulch it is."

It was an easy task to convince Colin of what was needed, although he complained mightily about being ganged up on by all the women in his life. What was more, he refused to let them go on their own and insisted on driving them.

"My pregnant wife and unborn child, and my overly confident sister, driving a cart two hours away to go shopping? Not on your life."

Within short order, Andrew's wife Melissa had been roped into keeping an eye on Anne while the three older Yorks went to Pepper Gulch. Natalie sighed happily as she took her seat in the back of the cart, arranging her skirts primly over her knees.

"You sure knew what you were doing when you asked Andrew and Melissa to come here and work for us, Colin. She's worth her weight in gold."

"Don't tell me you orchestrated this whole trip because you needed a break from your sweet, darling little girl," Colin called to her over his shoulder.

"All right – I won't tell you."

Mandy, sitting in the driver's box with her husband, laughed and slipped her arm through his. She rested her head against his shoulder.

"Is our little one going to be as full of fire as Anne is, do you think?"

"I don't see how it could be possible," said Colin. "I'm as mild as milk and sweet as pie."

The road to Pepper Gulch passed swiftly as the three laughed and joked together. Fleetingly, now and then, it crossed Natalie's mind that they might possibly see someone from the Flinn Ranch in Pepper Gulch, but she had enough self-control to avoid bringing it up. Anyhow, she knew what her brother would say if she did. *Someone? Just someone? Or a specific someone..."*

She was in too good of a mood to risk ruining it by Colin thinking he was funny. She kept her thoughts to herself and basked in the fresh spring air.

Only a week until the dance – how could time have flown by so quickly? It seemed just yesterday that Colin and Mandy had announced they were expecting, but it must have been a month. She wondered idly whether Crystal and Daphne were in charge of the food again this year. Of course, she was probably biased, but she was quite sure that last year must have been the best year ever as far as that went. She had thoroughly enjoyed everything about the county-wide get-together, from the food to the dancing...to the company.

A sudden memory of dancing closely with Emory flared through her mind, bringing an answering flare of heat to her cheeks.

She was grateful that her brother was looking the other way.

Before long, they were rolling into the town of Pepper Gulch. It was only big in comparison to South Meadows, but it struck Natalie how quickly she had adapted to things out here in the west. A town the size of Pepper Gulch would have only been called a hamlet back in West Virginia; it could hardly have even qualified for a village, let alone one of the largest towns in the county. But now that she had lived here over a year, she was finding that the press of buildings and the generous handfuls of people that lined the streets, busily going about their lives, was almost impressive compared to her day-to-day life on the ranch, where she saw only her family and the ranch hands.

Not that she would ever complain about that…

Well, not much, anyhow.

She practically leapt down from her seat once Colin finally rolled to a stop in front of the general store. She skipped around to take Mandy's hand and help her down.

"You've got errands to run yourself, don't you, Colin?"

He eyed her for a moment.

"As a matter of fact…"

"You don't want to come in with us," she assured him. "Believe me. We're going to look through every last ready-made and every last bolt of cloth, and pore over every last button and ribbon. You'd be bored out of your mind."

"Well, when you put it like that. I reckon I should go check in with Jim at the farrier's, haven't seen him a while and the mare could probably use new shoes before too long."

"Wonderful plan," said Natalie firmly, took her sister-in-law by the hand, and tugged her along after her, heading for the store. Mandy came willingly, though she was laughing.

"What was that all about?"

"Oh, I just know he'll be a stick in the mud about buying you dresses."

"Dresses. I'm only looking for the one."

"Mandy, you're going to be in this condition for some time. You need more than one dress. Besides..." She shrugged. "Suppose we happen to run into someone from Flinn Ranch. You know that it'll take that much longer if we see your sister – or someone – and Colin always gets fidgety when he has to wait for us."

"Oh, I should have tried to send word to Crystal and ask her if she would come in and meet us."

"It was too last minute. She could never have spared the time away from the baby, I'm sure. Don't feel bad." Natalie towed Mandy in the direction of the ready-made aisle, nodding a quick hello to Mr. Parmeter behind the counter. As the two began to comb through the clothing stacked on the shelves, holding them up one by one, she ventured, "Though I suppose they might be in here just by chance – maybe not Crystal, but maybe Ernest, or Daphne..."

"More likely to be Emory, I would think," said Mandy off-handedly, holding up a dress and scrutinizing it closely. "What do you think of this?"

"I think the pattern is lovely, but it will make it difficult to alter."

"Hmm. I think you're right."

"Why do you think it'd more likely be Emory?"

"Hmm?"

Natalie tried hard to keep her voice neutral. "I'm just curious why you think we'd more likely see Emory here in town than anyone else."

"Oh." Mandy dropped her hands and looked thoughtful. "He's been doing more and more for them off the ranch, rather than just being the foreman. I declare, it's almost like he's Ernest's brother living there, as close as they are. It makes me happy to know that Crystal has another dependable man around the place, just in case."

"Yes."

"He's such a good man, Emory is. And such a sad story – did you ever hear about what happened to his wife?"

Natalie felt as though her heart was about to leap out of her mouth. "His – wife?" she managed.

Mandy nodded, and lowered her voice. "I suppose he still doesn't talk about it much. I wouldn't know about it except Crystal told me when she found out. He was married for six or seven years, I guess, and his poor wife died so young. He lost the baby, too." She shook her head, putting a protective hand over her belly unconsciously. "Can you imagine, Natalie, losing both your wife and your baby at the same time? Going from a husband and a father to – to nothing. Just a man." She shook her head and sighed deeply. "It's such a tragedy for anyone to lose their entire family like that."

"That's awful," said Natalie quietly. She was staring deeply, unseeing, at a bolt of fabric. After a moment, Mandy reached over and put a hand on her shoulder.

"It's wise for all of us to remember," she said, "that everyone deals with some sort of pain. It's just that we don't always know. I'm sure your own pain from the past is as much a mystery to Emory as his is to you. That's why it's important to speak to each other, to get to know each other – so we can understand. The more we share our pain, the greater the feeling of relief becomes."

Natalie was unused to hearing such serious words from her sweet sister-in-law. She looked up at her, feeling a bit bewildered.

"What makes you say that?"

Mandy shook her head and smiled slightly.

"I know you fear the prospect of opening your heart again," she said. "I know that you feel you should be closed off to love, that Anne is your world now. But I think it's important to know that there is more going on than we think – just beneath the surface, every individual has the same sadness and needs and dreams that we do." She looked away, picking up another dress thoughtfully. "I saw you dancing with Emory, and some of the other men in the county, last year at the spring dance. But I know that you've made up your mind that love will never knock on your door again. And perhaps not."

Natalie fought back the tiny pinpricks of tears that came abruptly to her eyes at her sister-in-law's knowing words.

"Perhaps it will ring the bell," Mandy went on. She gave a small laugh. "Perhaps it'll just come right into your front room when you least expect it."

She lapsed into silence, letting her words sink in. Natalie tried to get ahold of herself, as her mind whirled with thoughts and questions and even the strong desire to ask Mandy for advice on what to do.

But finally, she managed to clear her mind, and her throat, and say a simple, "Thank you."

Mandy smiled at her.

"That's what sisters are for," she said.

It took some time to peruse the fabrics to their hearts content, but within a few hours they were finally able to locate both a dress that would be ideal for the dance the next week, as well as some more practical clothing that would suit Mandy as her figure grew and changed over the next several months. They took their selections to the counter and paid for them, chatting idly with Mr. Parmeter for a few moments.

Natalie found, to her dismay, that she kept looking around the store, as though expecting to see a familiar face—as though speaking about Emory Spencer would make him suddenly appear from behind the baking goods shelving. She shook her head at herself and told herself firmly that she must put him out of her mind – at least for now.

That was a big part of why it was so disconcerting to step back out into the street and see him going by in the Flinn Ranch farm cart.

It was unmistakably him. He wore no hat, and his dark hair was loosely windswept. He was so tall; it must be obvious to all and sundry who was driving the cart. To see him so unexpectedly after having spoken of him so intensely and intimately with Mandy made Natalie's stomach drop suddenly to her toes, while her heart seemed to soar up into the sky.

At the same time, that was only part of the shock. The other portion was the young woman who sat beside him in the driver's box of the cart. A very pretty young woman – a very *young* woman. She had dark hair and big dark eyes, and a sweet, heart-shaped face. She was small and slight and compact. She couldn't have been less like Natalie if she had specifically been trying, and she had her arm through that of Emory Spencer.

They had just gone by, but there was no mistaking what she had seen. She froze in mid-step, and Mandy, who was happily chatting about all her plans for her new purchases, didn't seem to notice, but walked a few steps on. By the time Mandy realized that Natalie had stopped dead where she stood, the Flinn Ranch farm cart was out of view around the corner, leaving only Natalie's white, fixed face and staring eyes.

"What?" Mandy asked, swiftly returning to her side. "What is it?"

Natalie shook her head quickly. She was already aflame with embarrassment; after just having been told that she should be ready to open her heart, and realizing that she was ready to do so, the last thing she wanted to do was tell her sister-in-law what she had just seen. It was too much; she couldn't confess to how the sight had affected her without also confessing how she had been feeling about Emory.

And she wasn't ready to do that. Not yet.

Perhaps not ever.

With the determination and sheer force of will that was common to her, she firmly pushed her emotions into a tiny little room at the back of her mind and shut the door on them.

She pulled herself together and faced Mandy full on.

"I thought I saw someone I recognized," she said, forcing her voice to resemble normalcy. "But I must have been wrong. Shall we walk down the street and find Colin? Are you up to a walk?"

"A walk sounds lovely," said Mandy. She let the questions in her eyes go unspoken, but it was clear that, as good as Natalie's acting was, she wasn't entirely convinced.

But that didn't matter, Natalie decided. She'd only reacted because it was so unexpected. Now that she knew it, she could pretend as though nothing had happened.

Now that she knew that Emory Spencer must have a sweetheart, someone close enough to him to put her arm through his and lean against his shoulder, she could pretend as though she had never cared much for him at all.

CHAPTER 7

As the season continued, the air warmed up. Setting the last shovelful of dirt in place and stamping it down to hold the fence post upright, Emory decided it was time to take a few moments for a break.

He stepped over into the shade of the lacy oak that spread over much of that corner of the far field, planted his back against it, and leaned his arms on the handle of the shovel. It was good to take a minute to survey the results of his hard work. The fence posts that were necessary for the new railings on this side were now all in place; over the next week or so, he and Ernest would tackle actually putting the railings securely into place, and then they could release the cattle back into this section of the land. It had been sitting untouched all through the winter; grass was already almost knee high in the good spring weather. Looking at it in wonder, Emory shook his head. It was amazing, he thought, how quickly things could grow.

Not six weeks before, this field had been hidden beneath a layer of snow. And all along, the grass seeds must have been there in the heart of it, just waiting for the touch of the sun…

He was still standing there musing over the poetic beauty of it all when he heard his name shouted from a distance. Turning his head curiously, he saw his sister coming his way with a little basket on one arm.

He leaned the shovel up against the tree and went to meet her.

She smiled at him sunnily as he approached.

"Cold tea… Crystal said you've got to be exhausted out here in the sun. Has it always been this hot and I just don't remember?" she asked.

"I reckon this is a hotter year than most. Come on over here in the shade. I expect she sent enough tea for you, too?"

"She did, at that."

They took seats on the grass just by the base of the tree trunk, and Emory leaned back against it while Almira busied herself with pulling the goods out of the basket. There was more than just a flagon of cold tea, of course; Crystal didn't do things by halves. She also sent bread and cheese.

"Mid-afternoon snack," Almira said cheerfully, handing it over to him. "Crystal says you've been working harder and harder these days."

"There's so much that needs to be done. And Ernest has a lot on his plate with Lina and the baby."

She nodded. "They're grateful to have you…no, don't 'aw, shucks' me, they really are. Crystal has told me so. Daphne, too.

Even Lina seems to realize how useful you are to her daddy. It makes me realize why you stayed behind to work when Ma and Pa and I left for Colorado – you were indispensable."

"Hardly that," said Emory, grinning. "I was just a delivery boy back then. Anyone can make deliveries."

"And now here you are, running a ranch. Ma and Pa would be proud."

"I hope they'll come and visit sometime, too."

She shrugged one shoulder. He watched her, wrinkling his brow in consternation.

"Was there some problem between you and them?"

"No…not a problem, exactly. They just – well, they never approved of John to begin with. So when he… you know… when he left – they didn't say it, but I knew they were thinking it. *I told you so.*" She sighed. "It's been frustrating to live with."

"They just care about you, that's all. They want you to be happy."

"I know it." She doubled her knees up and leaned on them, wrapping her arms around them, and looked up at the spreading branches of the tree. "Happiness seems like such a difficult thing to capture, doesn't it, Emory?"

"Sometimes it does, you're right. I wish I could tell you that it will get easier as you get older."

She dropped her head and glanced at him. For a moment she hesitated, evidently trying to choose her words with care.

"Emory – do you ever think about getting married again?"

He clenched his jaw, momentarily, and then forced himself to relax.

"I think about it," he said. "Sure. But do I actually believe that I would – not so much."

"But it's been three years…"

"I know. It isn't about the length of time that passes. It's about… oh, I dunno." He blew out his breath, thinking. "It's about…building trust again."

"Trust in who?"

"Myself, mostly."

She looked at him seriously. "Emory, what happened to Brigid and the baby was not your fault."

Unexpectedly, hot tears stung at the back of his eyes. He made a great effort and pushed them away, but he couldn't meet his little sister's gaze.

"I know it, Almi. But sometimes, it's hard to truly believe that," he said. He blew out his breath and his expression was solemn. "It's the same with you. What John did wasn't your fault. No one could have foreseen it or stopped it any more than you could have. No matter what Ma and Pa thought of him, there was nothing you could have done differently. So don't ever think it was your mistake. It wasn't. All right?"

She seemed taken aback by his sudden passionate words. He'd never been one for speaking what was going through his mind, but there it was, suddenly, all out in the open.

"All right," she said, and then rallied. "Neither of us were at fault for what happened to us."

"Right."

They sat for a moment, drinking their tea. Then she said, "I hope that you find someone else, Emory. You find someone, and I'll find someone, and we won't let our pasts stop us from finding our future."

He smiled at his hopeful little sister.

"Well, you'll have plenty of old friends from before coming around to dance with you this weekend, I reckon," he said, "so maybe you'll get your chance sooner than you think."

"For the party? Yes – I'm not sure how I feel about that. I don't want to be surrounded by strangers, because let's face it, I don't really know many people here anymore. But I do know I'll just feel sorry for myself if I stay at home. Besides, Lina asked me to dance with her." She chuckled.

"That's a start. Just don't fill up your dance card with all the kiddies, there'll be men lining up to take you for a spin around the floor."

"Will you go, Emory? Will you dance?"

For a moment he wavered between answering in the affirmative and answering with a decided no. Truth be told, he never knew from one moment to the next what he was going to do—despite having already brought it up with Natalie. He felt that strange shyness that pushed him to stay away from the crowd, and from her in particular. At the same time, he knew that if he went to the dance, he wouldn't want to dance with anyone other than that one person – and she would seek him out.

It was a fine line to walk, this building of trust.

Once he promised his sister one way or another, there was no going back. Besides, he could no longer pretend that he hadn't already committed himself to dancing with Natalie—he couldn't let her down.

He took hold of his courage with both hands, and said, "Yes. Yes, I will dance."

She smiled at him.

"Good." She stood up, taking the basket with her. "Crystal says don't forget to come for supper tonight." Almira turned to scrutinize the work he'd been doing. "Are you just about done putting up fences?"

Emory couldn't help but grin.

"Yes," he said. "Just about."

On the other side of the fence, the grass grew ever greener.

CHAPTER 8

The day of the spring dance dawned bright and clear. The way this season had been going, it was as though the clouds had finally forgotten how to form. The dreaded tornados had never appeared, only sending their threat ahead of them in the strange, still air. Now, Pepper Gulch seemed poised to leap straight into summertime, with only the barest hint of spring.

It certainly was hotter here than she ever remembered it being in West Virginia, Natalie thought, wiping her forehead with a handkerchief as the wagon rumbled toward Pepper Gulch.

She wondered if this was the way it would be from here on out. Would every year be sweltering from April to September? Was last year a blessed fluke? Was she doomed to live in discomfort for half of every year until she died?

She was glad she had enough self-control to keep her thoughts to herself. The others were chatting happily as they made their way to the dance; Colin and Mandy, Andrew and

Melissa, even little Anne was chatting, although to no one in particular. Everyone was bright and happy and beautifully dressed. Natalie alone felt as though there were a dark cloud hovering over her, and she didn't want to ruin the day for anyone else.

Not for the first time, she wondered whether coming to the dance at all was the right decision. Would she be able to take watching Emory and his new lady love dance the night away? The very thought of it filled her with bitterness – and regret.

But she had resolved to face up to it. She'd been looking forward to this dance for months—and mostly because of him. And she had agreed to dance with him, hadn't she? But now… Now, she didn't know what to think. The dance had been the highlight of last year. She wasn't about to let a failed romantic interest interfere with her enjoyment of the night…

No matter how hard she tried to push the thought away, it just kept coming back. The mental image, the memory of seeing Emory drive past with the little dark-haired girl leaning against him with such familiarity. It wasn't even that Emory must be involved with someone; it was that, to be so close, they must have had an understanding for some time. Which meant that each time Natalie had considered Emory as a potential suitor, he had more than likely already been attached…

Oh, it was embarrassing, and it just didn't bear thinking about.

So why couldn't she stop thinking about it?

Anne tapped her on the knee, demanding her attention, and she pulled her thoughts together and directed them to her child. Her beautiful darling, her angelic little girl, the apple of her eye – the reminder of so much pain. Natalie couldn't explain it – it wasn't as though Emory had ever said anything to her about courting her, after all – but it felt suddenly as though she had been rejected all over again, just as had happened with Anne's father.

She pulled the little girl close to her at the thought, reminding herself how grateful she was that Anne was healthy and happy… and demanding that Natalie make Uncle Coll stop the cart so the horsey could pick an apple.

Natalie suppressed her laughter, as she could tell Colin and Mandy were doing as well.

"Darling, horses don't pick apples, I don't think."

"But he's hungry. I can tell."

There was no arguing with a two-year-old's logic. After much back and forth on the subject, Natalie agreed that pulling a wagon probably did adversely affect the ability of a horse to do as they wished, whether that wish actually involved picking an apple or not. The only way she was able to wiggle out of the discussion was by finally pointing out to Anne that the only trees in sight would not bear apples, but acorns, and that the horse didn't much like acorns.

Anne sat back in her seat and crossed her arms, descending into a sulk. "But he's hungry."

"I hate to say it," Natalie observed to her brother and sister-in-law, "but I almost miss the days when she was just making nonsense noises with Lina."

The mention of her favorite cousin made Anne brighten up considerably, and the rest of the ride was much calmer as the little girl jabbered on about Lina. It also had the effect of temporarily distracting Natalie from her own sulk, so when they finally pulled to a stop in Pepper Gulch before the town hall and all stepped out of the wagon, Mandy took her arm and smiled at her.

"I'm glad to see you smile," she said. "You finally look as though you're ready for the dance."

"Did I not look ready before?" Natalie arched her eyebrows.

"No," said Mandy frankly. "As a matter of fact, you haven't seemed like yourself all week. You're hardly smiling, you never laugh, and you're not even arguing with Colin, even when he goes out of his way to provoke you. We were beginning to get worried." She scrutinized Natalie's face. "You are better – aren't you? Is something still wrong?"

Natalie shook her head, but it was evident that Mandy wasn't going to take this for an answer.

"Is it about Anne?" she asked, lowering her voice. "I know you were concerned about bringing her into town – it's the first time you've had her here in Pepper Gulch with you."

Natalie stopped dead, the realization washing over her that she had been so caught up in thoughts of Emory and his girl that she had scarcely even given a thought to what might happen as she brought her daughter into the public eye for the first time. She tried to wrap her brain around it, confused and bewildered at herself. She had spent the entirety of the last year avoiding being seen with Anne in Pepper Gulch, hiding from the questions that inevitably followed. Those hurtful questions and, worse, accusations had been a large part of the reason why she and Colin had decided to leave West Virginia before Anne was even a year old. The community that had known Natalie from when she was a child did not have enough confidence in her to trust that she was a decent and loyal young woman; what chance had she in convincing this crowd of relative strangers that she and her daughter did not deserve their ostracism?

Or, even worse, was there no chance to convince them? Would the fact that she was an unmarried mother, with a child born out of wedlock, be more than enough to color her in their eyes, regardless of any explanation that might be given?

And how was it – how on earth was it possible – that she had been so consumed with thoughts of Emory Spencer that she had not even thought of this until now?

For a moment she hesitated, poised to flee.

"Perhaps this was a mistake," she mumbled.

Mandy gripped her shoulder.

"Don't think like that," she said. "What's done is done, and you and Anne have your new beginning here. You shouldn't have to hide out forever because you fear what they might say."

Natalie shook her head, but Colin stepped up and put his arm around his little sister.

"We knew this day would come," he said quietly. It was obvious that he had caught most, if not all, of the conversation between his wife and his sister. "It isn't fair to you or Anne to try to keep it in the dark. Let them say what they want to say – they'll get over it. And you're not doing this alone, Natalie – your family is here with you, and we are proud to be at your side."

Natalie found her eyes drawn to Anne, who was prancing impatiently a few feet away, waiting to go in to find Lina and start to dance.

Colin squeezed her comfortingly. "I'm proud to be at your side," he said again, in a whisper.

Natalie took a deep breath and nodded.

"You're right. This has to be done sooner or later – I've already waited a year. Poor Anne shouldn't be kept at home because her mother is afraid."

Mandy took her hand and squeezed it.

"You're not afraid of anything," she said quietly. "You're Natalie York – the bravest woman I know."

Together, they went into the town hall.

It was decked out even more beautifully than she remembered it being last year. There were flowers and grasses everywhere she looked, wreathes and banners and candles and oil lamps, setting the whole of the hall aglow. Anne spotted Lina in the distance and took off toward her, going as fast as she could on her chubby steps. Lina swooped her up and the two immediately fell back into their odd, comfortable communication of strange noises back and forth —although Natalie heard quite a bit of regular talk thrown in. Mandy squeezed Natalie's hand one last time and allowed Colin to lead her off to the dance floor. Natalie stood alone for a moment, looking over the packed hall.

This was Pepper Gulch – this was the place where she had decided to make her life, come what may. She had her brother, her family, her little girl. She had her hopes and dreams for the future. She might never love or be loved again by a man, but that didn't mean she wasn't loved.

And she knew then that she had nothing to fear.

The next second, that surge of confidence was put to the test by the sight of Emory Spencer, with the slight, dark-haired girl standing very close to him. They were talking about something and laughing together.

Natalie felt a bitter taste on her tongue, but she swallowed it, drew herself up, squared her shoulders, and marched in their direction.

If she had nothing to fear from Pepper Gulch, she had nothing to fear from Emory Spencer, either. No, he might not want her – but their friendship was still in place, and she wasn't so callous as to completely devalue that friendship simply because she'd let her feelings run away with her.

Her stomach was twisting into knots. But she wasn't about to let her body dictate whom she spoke with.

Striving for as much of a normal tone and smile as she could manage, she called out to Emory as she approached. "Good evening, Emory."

The foreman of Flinn Ranch looked around. If she wasn't mistaken, his eyes lit up when he saw her. There was enough joy on his face, a particular sort of joy, to throw her into confusion. What on earth was happening?

"Natalie. Come here and meet Almira."

Gritting her teeth slightly, she came all the way forward. The dark-haired girl – Almira – reached a hand out to her eagerly, smiling. Goodness, she was so young. Could that be the reason why Emory had looked elsewhere – because of Natalie's age? The very thought made her feel wretched.

Nevertheless, she clasped hands with the girl, managing to hold on to her smile.

"Good evening."

"Hello, Natalie. I'm pleased to meet you at last – if I'm not mistaken, Emory's mentioned you a time or two in his letters." She slid her eyes sideways at Emory, who blushed a little and scratched the back of his neck with one hand.

"Could be, could be…"

"You two have been exchanging letters?" said Natalie.

"Sure," said Emory. "We like to keep up with each other on what's happening. I've been waiting for her to come and visit since I moved back from Colorado."

"You know I couldn't until now," said Almira, nudging him with her elbow.

"You could have come any time you wanted. You just didn't miss me enough."

Natalie remained determined to keep her good relationship with her friend; however, it was just too much to ask her to take this affectionate teasing.

"Are you staying at the ranch?"

"Yes," said the girl. "Crystal was kind enough to put me up in the spare room, since there isn't really enough room in the cottage."

"There's enough room," said Emory defensively. "She just didn't want you to feel crowded, that's all."

"Maybe she was worried we wouldn't get along," said Almira, and the two chuckled.

This was verging on the scandalous, in Natalie's opinion. She eyed them, trying to decide whether it was all an elaborate joke of some sort. Emory certainly didn't seem like the type to play tricks; on the other hand, neither did he seem like the sort to joke about inviting an unmarried woman to stay in his quarters.

"Either way, they're glad to have you," Emory told Almira, smiling down at her. "I hope you sent word to Ma and Pa to let them know that you're being taken care of." He turned to Natalie, "It's not every day that your little sister comes all the way from Colorado to visit," he said. "I guess I'm just glad that our parents let her make the trip."

Suddenly, everything fell into place.

"Your sister," said Natalie faintly. "She's your sister."

"Yes..." Emory squinted at her. "I guess I should have said, but..."

"Your sister." Natalie shook her head. Suddenly she was angry, very angry at herself. Why was she crying? This was stupid. "Of course."

Emory reached out and laid a tentative hand on her arm.

"Natalie..."

"I don't know why I..."

"Natalie, what did you think..."

Almira, with a clarity and wisdom that seemed beyond her years, gave her older brother a gentle shove.

"I think," she said, "you two should go and dance."

CHAPTER 9

Without protest, her head in a whirl, Natalie York allowed Emory Spencer to lead her onto the dance floor. It was a less energetic reel than some of them, for which she was grateful. She really didn't think she had the composure to remember all the steps and follow through on the movements without help. But Emory, for all he claimed not to be a good dancer, guided her through the movements gently, and in between, as they had a few moments standing next to each other, he murmured, "Are you all right?"

"Yes…" she gasped, though she wasn't entirely sure herself. "I think so."

"You thought Almira was…"

"I don't know what I thought."

She caught his grin. "Well, now, I dunno that I believe that to be true," he said.

Natalie realized suddenly that though her heart was pounding, it was also soaring.

"Let's just dance for a moment," she said.

The next few moments were a dizzying spin of his eyes, fixed on hers, and the careful touch of his warm, avid hands. As the tune came to a spirited end, she reached out and took his hand, and he led her to a quiet corner where they could talk.

"You're right," she said. "I do know what I thought. I thought she was your betrothed, or that you were at least attached…"

"Well, we are attached. We're brother and sister." He grinned. "Just a different sort of attachment than what I feel for you."

"Emory, please don't joke at a time like… Wait. What do you mean?"

"Hmm?" He shrugged, affecting innocence. She gripped hard onto his shoulder.

"What do you mean, the attachment that you feel for me?"

"Oh, Miss Natalie," he said, as he chuckled, shook his head, and sighed. "Are you sure we shouldn't go back out and dance a little more? Maybe if I give you a little time to think about it, you'll reach the conclusion all on your own."

She gave him a look, but he only smiled at it, took her hand, and led her back toward the music. He didn't pull her into the middle of the dance floor this time, for which she was grateful. Together, they danced at the edge of the tumult, where things were a little quieter.

She glanced over at the crowd at the sound of a child's happy laughter, and caught sight of Anne and Lina, dodging around the spinning couples, having the time of their life. She couldn't help but smile.

As she locked hands with Emory, she caught a series of chatter from not too far away, though once she did, she regretted it.

"Such a pretty girl, but hard, proud. You can understand how someone like that can get themselves in trouble."

"But I didn't realize she had a child…who does it belong to?"

Another few words that she couldn't quite make out. Natalie was conscious of a growing coldness in the pit of her stomach.

The voices were louder for a moment.

"York – she doesn't go by a married name because she *hasn't* a married name."

"The father must have left…"

"I heard she claimed it was her fiancé, but he denied it and fled the state to get away from the slander."

"Did you hear that from their previous ranch hand? That's who was spreading the news. Well, I can't imagine…"

"The poor child, it isn't *her* fault that her mother made such unwise decisions."

Natalie stopped dead, feeling everything go frozen and still. Dear Lord have mercy, did the women not see her so close by? She looked into Emory's eyes, frantically; it was clear by the discomfort in them that he had heard as clearly as she had. As she searched his gaze, his eyes wavered and fell to the side.

Natalie's heart plummeted – it felt as though her heart had left her outright, so far away that she would never get it back.

That was what she got for trusting.

This was all she had ever deserved.

Her eyes misting over, she dropped Emory's hands, practically tossing them away from her, and rushed for the door, pushing past the joyous dancers, seeking only to get away.

Outside, the sun had finally sunk behind the horizon, and the twilight was stretching long purple fingers everywhere she looked. The town of Pepper Gulch was empty, and the crowd was there behind her. She was alone – she had always been alone.

No one would ever be proud to stand beside her. Relying on people only led to disaster and tragedy.

She folded her arms around her and began to walk.

Blinded by tears, she did not move very quickly. She could hear nothing but the pounding of her heart in her ears. She had faced the crowd, all right – and they had cut her down. She had been brave, but sometimes being brave only ended in harm. Her heart ached for little Anne, blissfully unaware of what the grownup whispers might mean; but it also ached for herself.

She had been so innocent, so easily misled. She could hate her younger self for being so foolish, but there was no point in it. All she could do from now on was steel herself never to let it happen again – never to let anyone into that position of trust, from which they could harm her.

"Natalie – Natalie!"

Emory's voice broke over her like a wave, and then he was at her side, a hand on her arm, pulling her to face him. His face was earnest, and his voice was strained, but calm, as though it were costing him a great effort to remain so.

"Don't run from me, Natalie."

"I'm not running from you," she said sadly, shaking her head. "I just didn't want you to have to ask me to leave you alone – not after what we heard."

Emory huffed out a breath. He released her arm and spread his arms out in an uncharacteristically grand gesture.

"Do you think I care what they say about you?" he cried. "Do you think I didn't know that you had some sadness in your past? We all do, Natalie – you, me, poor Anne. Colin, Ernest – all of us. Do you think I would reject you, as though what happened had damaged you beyond saving?" He took a deep breath, regaining control of himself. Slowly, he lowered his arms and brought his hands to rest on her waist. "There's always a better way," he whispered to her.

"What is it?" she asked him, voice low and broken.

"Love," Emory told her. He pulled her toward him gently. "Love is always the better way. Always the right choice."

She could not stop the tears from flowing now, but he didn't seem to care. He kissed her forehead, then gently below each eye, and finally her lips. They stood together in the reigning twilight, until she finally reached up with shaking hands and wrapped her arms around his neck.

"It doesn't matter what those two biddies say about you," Emory murmured to her. "They're just a few – they don't speak for the town. It's too bad if they don't understand, or if they don't have the compassion they should. But you can't write off the whole of Pepper Gulch because of them. And me – I will never turn you away." He pulled back a little and looked into her eyes. "Haven't you figured that out yet?"

"Tell me?"

"I love you, Natalie York. I never thought I'd be able to say those words again, but they're the truth. And the truth should always be said."

She was still crying; but they were happier tears, now.

She pulled him close, burying her face against his neck.

"Everyone around me had their happy endings," she said. "I had made up my mind that I would just enjoy the happiness of my brother, of my friends. I had made up my mind that I didn't need anything for myself."

"Well, make up your mind again," he said. "Are you going to marry me?"

Natalie lifted her head, smiling like a ray of sunshine through the clouds.

"If I say yes," she said, "will you dance with me again?"

Emory grinned, and took her by the hand. They walked back toward the town hall, with the light and the music and the movement and the crowd, proud to be walking hand in hand. Proud to be standing together.

Proud and grateful to see their future start to unfold…

The End

CONTINUE READING...

Thank you for reading *Natalie's Ranch Hand!* Are you wondering **what to read next?** Why not read *The Reluctant Groom?* **Here's a peek for you:**

The bitterly cold wind sliced through her thin cloak as she walked through the darkness. Her bare hand, rapidly turning numb, clutched the wool to her throat, and kept her hood over her head. Exhausted from her day's labor, Halley trudged toward home, visualizing the welcome she'd receive.

Lord, if you're listening, don't let him invite yet another suitor for the evening.

Though she walked through a neighborhood in Philadelphia not known for its prosperity or well-to-do residents, Halley didn't fear to be out with no escort. Any thugs living nearby went to richer areas of the city to plunder or rob. Known to be as poor as anyone else, Halley had little for a robber to steal.

Smoke drifted upward from the chimney of the small house surrounded by a picket fence that once upon a time had been white. The smoke blew away under the brisk wind, yet the lights streaming from the windows welcomed her home. Still, she wished she had anywhere else to go except here.

"I'm home," she called, closing the front door behind her.

Removing her cloak to hang it on the peg, Halley continued to shiver as she rubbed her icy hand, trying to bring life back to it. The house wasn't a great deal warmer than outside, but at least the wind couldn't enter. Spencer tended to be miserly regarding firewood.

"In here," he bellowed. "About time, girl."

Halley ventured around the corner to the small front room, dismay seizing her by her throat. Spencer Coldwell, her godfather and guardian, glowered from his wing-backed armchair close to hearth. He didn't stand at her entrance, but a pair of young men did.

"We're hungry," Spencer snapped, snugly wrapped in a blanket. "Get the stove lit and dinner made. Be quick about it."

Bitter bile rose to her mouth, but Halley swallowed it back. The two men, brothers, Robert and Ronald Landon, didn't smile. They leered. Both of them utterly disgusted her with their lack of manners, their squat and heavy bodies, their foul body odors. Both sought her hand in marriage.

Spencer appeared adamant that Halley marry one of them.

"Good to see you again, Miss Englewood," Robert said, his brown teeth bared in what passed for him as a smile.

"Yeah, Miss Englewood," Ronald added. "How are you?"

Visit HERE To Read More!

https://ticahousepublishing.com/mail-order-brides.html

ABOUT THE AUTHOR

Susannah has always been intrigued with the Western movement - prairie days, mail-order brides, the gold rush, frontier life! As a writer, she's excited to combine her love of story with her love of all that is Western. Presently, Susannah lives in Wyoming with her hubby and their three amazing children.

www.ticahousepublishing.com
contact@ticahousepublishing.com